FLEET-FOOTED FLORENCE

FLEET-FOOTED FLORENCE

A sequel to MATT'S MITT

by Marilyn Sachs
illustrated by Charles Robinson

Doubleday & Company, Inc., Garden City, New York

Library of Congress Catalog Card Number 76-56330
ISBN: 0-385-12745-6 Trade
ISBN: 0-385-12746-4 Prebound
Text copyright © 1981 by Marilyn Sachs
Illustrations copyright © 1981 by Charles Robinson
All Rights Reserved
Printed in the United States of America
First Edition

For my uncle, Ben Rosenberg —
"The Old Professor of Sports"

Matt, the famous baseball hero, had three sons. He hoped that they would become baseball players too.

The first one was named Willie M., after the great hitter. But the only thing Willie M. was great at hitting was his younger brother.

The second one was named Lou B. after the great base stealer. But Lou B. was only great at stealing cookies from the cookie jar.

The third one was named Johnny B., after the great catcher. But the only thing Johnny B. ever caught was colds.

Matt had a daughter too. He didn't expect *her* to become a baseball player, so he called her Florence N., after the great nurse.

One day, there was a fire a few blocks away from where Matt lived. Matt stood on the porch and watched. First, he saw the fire engines go by. Then he saw the police car go by. Then he watched the neighborhood kids run by. He saw Willie M. and Lou B. and Johnny B. Then he saw a blue whoosh.

"What," he asked a neighbor, "was that blue whoosh?"
"That blue whoosh," replied the neighbor, "was your daughter, Florence."

Then Matt knew that his daughter, Florence N., would grow up to be a baseball player.

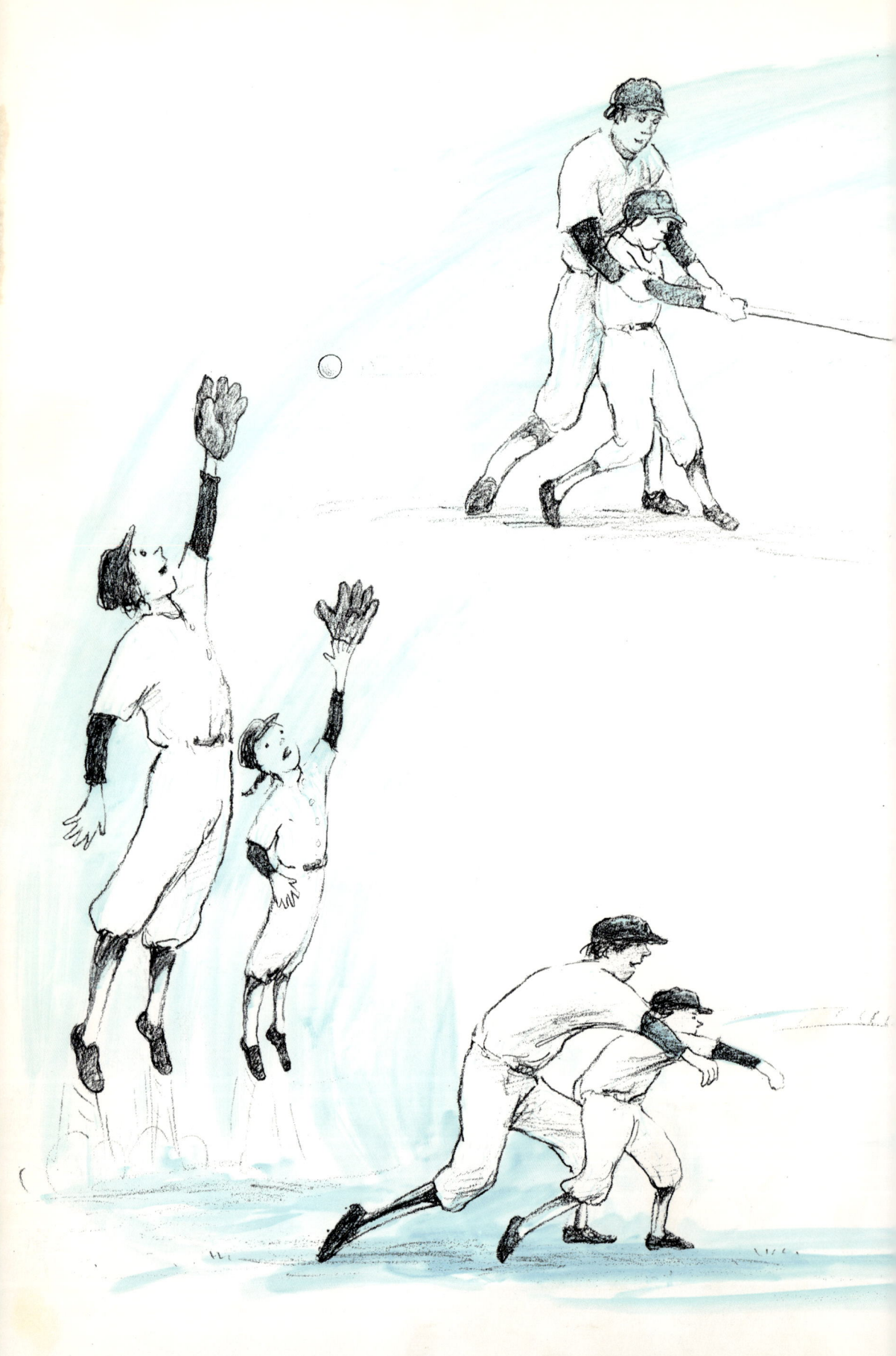

Matt taught her how to hit.
And he taught her how to catch.
He taught her how to throw.
But he did not have to teach her
how to run.

When Florence N. grew up, she went to
play on her father's old team, The North
Dakota Beavers. They had won thirteen
World Series in a row in the days Matt played for them.
But ever since he left, they had been in a slump.

Florence changed all that.
She was the fastest runner in the West.
And the fastest runner in the East.
The fastest runner in the North.
And the fastest runner in the South.

Nobody ever ran as fast as Florence.
When she came up to bat, everybody on the opposing team trembled. Because they knew that once she got on base, if there was nobody in front of her, she would come home.

Her fans called her FLEET-FOOTED FLORENCE, and every game you could hear them shout: HOORAY FOR FLEET-FOOTED FLORENCE!

But her enemies called her FLAT-FOOTED FLORENCE
or FAT-HEADED FLORENCE, and often both.
Every game, you could hear them shout:
PHOOEY ON YOU, FAT-HEADED, FLAT-FOOTED FLORENCE

Florence played centerfield. She could run faster than the ball. So when she caught it, if there was a runner trying to advance after the catch, she generally ran in to tag him out.

She specialized in four outs. Whenever the bases were loaded, and she caught a fly ball, she liked to run in and personally tag each player out as he returned to his base.

Sometimes her enemies called:
BREAK A LEG, FLAT-FOOTED FLORENCE!

She did once, tripping over a beer can
flung on the field. But she played anyway.
And stole two bases instead of three, and
put only three men out instead of four.

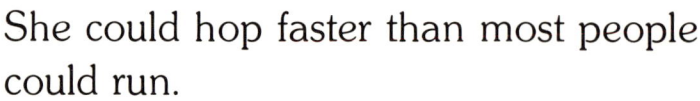

She could hop faster than most people
could run.
Sometimes when her team was leading, she
would play with one leg tied behind her back.

The North Dakota Beavers won the pennant the first year Florence came to play on their team. And that year, they faced their old enemies, the New York Yankees, in the world series.

Now the mightiest Yankee of all was Fabulous Frankie, the magnificent catcher. Frankie could catch, and Frankie could hit, and Frankie could throw.

But Frankie could not run as fast as Florence.
And Frankie had a habit of hitting balls
out toward centerfield.
Which meant that Florence made more four
outers off Frankie's fly balls than off
anybody else's.

This made Frankie angry — very angry, very, very, angry! So angry, in fact, that he flipped. Every time Florence caught his fly balls or tagged out his teammates, or stole three bases under his nose, he flipped. He flipped so much that he became known as: FRANKIE, THE YANKEE FLIPPER

The worst thing was that he lost his cool.
He lost his appetite too, and he lost his
sleep. He started letting pitches get by him,
and North Dakota Beaver fans began yelling:
FUMBLE-FINGERED FRANKIE, THE YANKEE
FLIPPER YAA! YAA! YAA!
Nobody called him Fabulous anymore.

One day, after the Beavers had won their third World Series game off the Yankees, and were trying for their fourth, Florence hit a tiny, baby bunt, and came flying around the bases into home plate just as Frankie was picking it up.

They met head on.
Eyeball to eyeball.
It was the first time they had ever been
so close to one another.

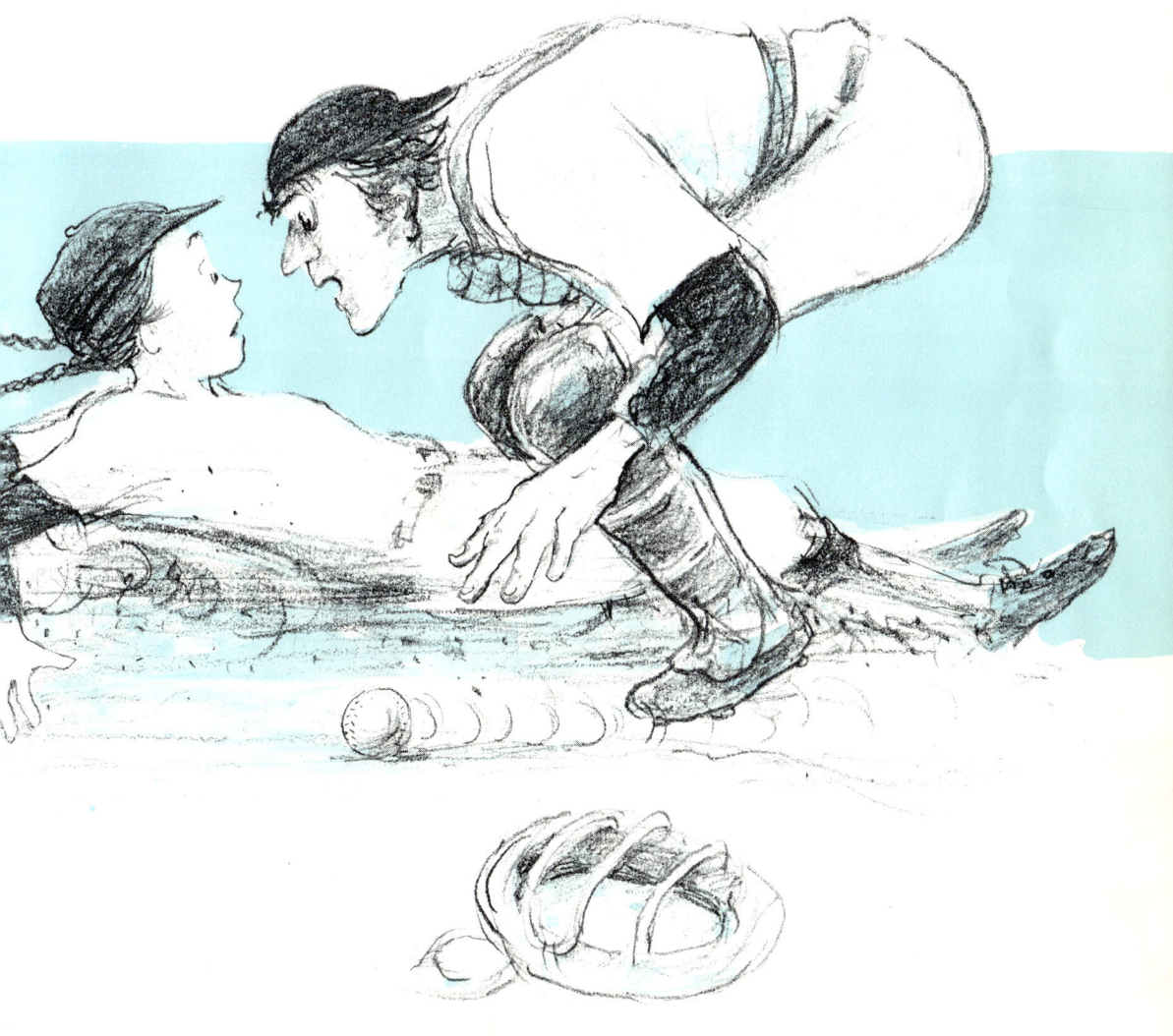

After that, Frankie didn't seem to mind
when Florence made four outs off his fly balls.
And sometimes, Florence even counted to
ten before she ran in and made her four outs.

was in all the papers.

FLEET-FOOTED FLORENCE FLIPS OVER FABULOUS FRANKIE

Soon after, they got married.

Frankie was traded to The North Dakota Beavers, and he and Florence became the most famous pair of lovers in baseball history. They did live happily ever after too, but that is not the end of the story.

Florence set so many records that there was no book big enough to hold them all. Most great baseball players become famous because of their RBI's* or ERA's** or just their BA's***. Florence, alone, is also famous for being the only player to have an outstanding record of RCI's****.

*Runs batted in
**Earned run average
***Batting average
****Runs carried in

Of course, she had to make sure that each player she carried in touched each base before she did.

One day, an old woman, dressed in a shabby baseball cap and jacket, stood outside the dugout asking for autographs. All the other players hurried by, except for Florence.

She smiled at the old woman.
She inquired after her health.
And she autographed her scorecard.
"Fleet-footed Florence," said the old woman, "you are the greatest baseball star who ever lived."
"Ah," sighed Florence, "I wish I might always be a star."

The old woman drew out from under her warm-up jacket a golden baseball. "Because you are good and kind as well as a great star, I have it in my power to grant you your wish."

Then the old woman threw the ball with all her might, and Florence said, "Never fear, Ma'am, I will retrieve that ball for you."

So saying, she hurried after the glittering ball. Faster and faster it rolled, and faster and faster Florence ran after it. Out of the stadium, through the parking lot, and over the city streets spun the golden ball. Right behind it came Florence, laughing in the joy of the race. And right behind Florence, came Frankie, crying, "Florence, wait for me!"

Suddenly, the ball rose up into the sky, and Florence reached back for Frankie, and leaped.

Florence was never seen again. Neither was Frankie. Some say they have retired into the country and are raising a family of future ballplayers — five girls and four boys.

Some say they are traveling incognito, and can be seen scouting every sand lot where future ballplayers are most likely to be found. Maybe so.

But I think you should look carefully up
at the sky on a clear night. Do you really think
that flashing, glittering light that moves
faster than anything else up there is only
a shooting star? Watch! Here it comes again,
and see, it really is not a shooting star.
You know who it really is racing across the
heavens, carrying Frankie in her arms, flying
faster than the moon, faster than the sun,
faster than any of the other stars.

Fleet-footed Florence, for all time now,
the fastest star in the firmament.